# FINE LINES

*by*

## Ruth Heller

*photographs by*

## Michael Emery

Richard C. Owen Publishers, Inc.
Katonah, New York

## Meet the Author titles

Text copyright © 1996 by The Ruth Heller Trust
Photographs copyright © 1996 by Michael Emery

Richard C. Owen Publishers, Inc.
PO Box 585
Katonah, New York 10536

Library of Congress Cataloging-in-Publication Data

Heller , Ruth , 1924-
        Fine lines / by Ruth Heller ;  photographs by Michael Emery .
        p .   cm .  — (Meet the author   Katonah , N. Y. )
        Summary:  A children's book illustrator shares her daily routine and creative life ,
showing how the two are intertwined.
        ISBN 1-878450-76-X :
        1 .  Heller , Ruth , 1924-  — Juvenile literature .  2 . Illustrators —
United States — Biography — Juvenile literature .  3 . Illustrated
books , Children's — United States — Juvenile literature .
        [ 1 .  Heller , Ruth , 1924-    2 . Illustrators. . 3 . Illustration of books. ]
I . Emery , Michael , ill . II . Title . III . Series .
NC975.5.H47A2  1996
741.6'42'092—dc 20
[B]

                                                                                    96-15440
                                                                                         CIP
                                                                                          AC

Editorial, Art, and Production Director    *Janice Boland*
Production Assistant    *Matthew Vartabedian*
Color separations by Leo P. Callahan Inc., Binghamton, NY

Printed in the United States of America

9 8 7 6 5 4 3

Every Day is

Earth Day

To Janice and Michael,
my talented team

I live with my husband Richard
on top of a hill in San Francisco, California.
I love my beautiful home with its magical view.

My studio is at the bottom of another hill. It overlooks San Francisco Bay. It's messy and cluttered, and I love it, too. It's full of books, and drawings, and projects that children have made for me. It's where most of my ideas begin and where most of my research and all of my illustrations are done.

I was born in Winnipeg, Manitoba, Canada on April
2, 1923.  But my father wanted to find a new place
for our family to live.  He traveled to many cities
and countries and decided he liked San Francisco
the best.  Here he is in Egypt on a camel.

When I was one year old, my mother, father, brother Daniel, and I moved to Vancouver, on the west coast of Canada, to await our turn to enter the United States. We waited ten years.

Vancouver is beautiful.  I loved to play on its
beaches and collect shells.  In my books I draw
shells and fish and underwater scenes a lot.

We lived on King Edward
Avenue and I went to Prince of
Wales School.  In Canada, streets
are often named after British
kings and queens and princes
and princesses.  Maybe that's
why I put them in my books.

But if inside *already* is what you really mean . . .
then . . . eating bread and honey . . .

in
the parlor
is the queen.

Our house had terraces and lawns
and roses and berries and fruit
trees.  In the spring, a huge
willow tree was covered with
caterpillars.  I collected them
in jars full of leaves, punched
holes in the lids so they could
breathe, and hoped they would
change into butterflies.  Not
many did.  I wonder if that's
why there are so many
butterflies in my books.

On summer evenings, we took drives through the park and stopped to buy Eskimo Pies. Don't be surprised if an Eskimo Pie shows up soon in one of my books.

I've always loved to color and draw,
and cut and paste, and make things.
And I've always loved to read.
My favorite books were legends and fairy tales,
so isn't it strange that all the books I write are
nonfiction? I took art whenever I could in junior
high and high school. In college, I studied
painting and art history. I graduated with a Fine
Arts degree from the University of California.

After my two sons Paul and Philip were in school,
I studied drawing and design at the California
College of Arts and Crafts. My first job after that
was designing gift wrapping
and other paper products
and newspaper ads. As a
freelance designer, I created
many posters and puzzles
and coloring books.

In the late 1970s, I got an idea for a children's book. For years, nobody would publish it! So in 1980, I spent the month of May in Saratoga Springs, New York, at a place where artists and writers work called Yaddo. There, I rewrote my story and created six spreads. A spread consists of two pages that face each other when a book is open. A publisher in New York City liked it and *Chickens Aren't the Only Ones*, my first picture book, was published in 1981. I have been writing and illustrating children's books ever since.

Yaddo

14

When I am creating a book, I work long hours every day. My studio is a seven-minute drive from my home. By 6:30 A.M., I am at work. I stop for lunch, to run errands, and to get some exercise.

At the end of the day, my head is still full
of words and pictures and ideas.  I like
to unwind by working on a crossword puzzle
before falling asleep.

On weekends I sleep late, have breakfast in bed, work in my studio from noon to six, and spend the evening with my family and friends.

When a deadline gets close, I stay in my studio
until I'm finished.  I work late into the night
and sometimes don't go home at all.
Richard keeps me company.

I have always been fascinated with words.
That's probably why I write books about nouns
and adjectives and verbs and adverbs and
prepositions.  I have a wonderful rhyming
dictionary and a collection of other dictionaries
to help me find the words I want.

I collect things that attract me and often
use them in my illustrations. At Mardi Gras
in New Orleans one year, I bought some beautiful
feather masks. You can see them on the cover
of my book about prepositions called
*Behind the Mask*.

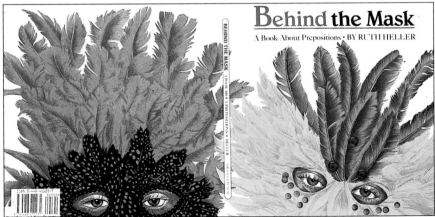

My illustrations require time and patience.
Friends and relatives often act as models for me.
I start all my drawings on tracing paper.
Sometimes I take forever to make a drawing look
exactly the way I want it.  That can be frustrating.
Sometimes it's easy, and that's fun.

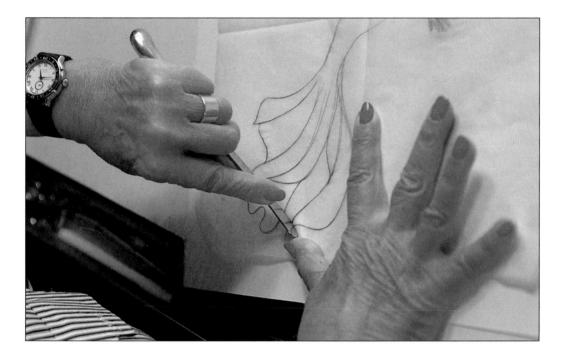

I transfer my drawings to smooth watercolor paper by turning the tracing paper over and rubbing on the lines with a butter knife or a Popsicle stick. I learned to do that in second grade, and it still works for me.

I trace over my pencil lines in ink, and then I color with markers and colored pencils. I have always been fascinated with color. My book *Color* has transparencies in it so that you can see how all colors in any book are made from only four basic colors.

The printer is some kind of wizard, I think.

In miniscule dots he applies all the ink. He applies all the ink to a surface that's white.

HOKUS and POKUS— Behold! What a sight!

I prefer to write and illustrate my own books, but I have illustrated five books for other authors. When I illustrated the book *The Korean Cinderella* by Shirley Climo, I traveled to Korea to learn about the costumes, the architecture, the landscape, and the culture of that country. It was a wonderful experience.

When I have completed a book, I fly to New York.
It is an exciting moment for me when I finally
show my editor and art director in New York City
what I have been working on in San Francisco.

I visit schools and talk to students about my books and give presentations to teachers and librarians at conferences.

This means that I have to travel a great deal.
Some people say I travel too much,
but I don't think so. I love it!
I get lots of writing and thinking done at airports
and on planes, where I am not distracted
by phone calls or daily chores.

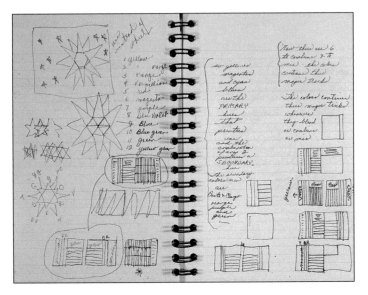

I carry a notebook, a pen, and a few colored pencils with me so that I can jot down ideas and make quick sketches. Nobody else in the whole world would be able to understand them because they look like this:

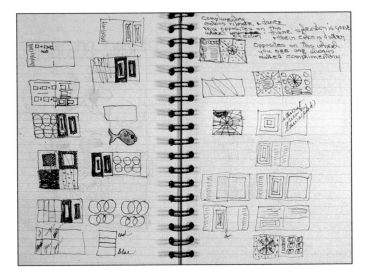

love my beautiful home with its magical view.

My studio is at the bottom of another hill. It overlooks San Francisco Bay. It's messy and cluttered, and I love it too. It's full of books and art supplies and drawings and projects that children have made for me. It's where most of my ideas begin, and where most of my research and all of my illustrations are done.

Both are far from where I was born in Winnipeg, Manitoba, Canada on April 2, 1923

My mother, father, brother, Daniel and I moved to Vancouver, on the west coast of Canada, when I was one year old.

I do not have a word processor or a typewriter. I do all my writing in longhand. And I write on anything…but usually in a notebook.

I love talking with children about my work

and showing them my illustrations.

"Why do you write in rhyme?" they often ask.
"I don't know," I reply,
"but I write in rhyme all the time."
I can't say that any more.
This book is written in prose.

"Do you suppose
I might compose
more
prose?
Who knows?"

## Other Books by Ruth Heller

*Animals Born Alive and Well; Kites Fly High: A Book about Verbs; Many Luscious Lollipops: A Book about Adjectives; Merry-go-round: A Book about Nouns; Up Up and Away: A Book about Adverbs*

## About the Photographer

Michael Emery is a documentary and editorial photographer. His first book was *From Dry Dock To D-Day: The Return Voyage of the SS Jeremiah O'Brien*. Michael holds a Fine Art degree in photography from The College of Art in San Francisco. Currently he is working with Jane Goodall on a video about her *Roots and Shoots* program for children. Michael and his wife live in San Francisco, California.

## Acknowledgments

*Every Day is Earth Day* poster on dedication page illustrated by Ruth Heller appears courtesy of Scholastic Inc. Photographs on pages 6, 7, 10, 11, top of page 13, page 17, page 23, bottom of page 24, 31, and back cover courtesy of Ruth Heller. Illustration at top of page 8 from *Merry-go- round: A Book about Nouns* by Ruth Heller. Copyright 1990 by Ruth Heller. Grosset & Dunlap, Inc. Illustration at bottom of page 8 courtesy of Ruth Heller from *The Big Book for Our Planet*. Illustration on page 9 from *Behind the Mask: A Book about Prepositions* by Ruth Heller. Copyright 1995 by Ruth Heller. Grosset & Dunlap, Inc. Illustrations on pages 10 and 14 from *Chickens Aren't the Only Ones* by Ruth Heller. Copyright 1981 by Ruth Heller. Grosset & Dunlap, Inc. Illustration on page 19 of front and back covers of *Behind the Mask: A Book about Prepositions* by Ruth Heller. Copyright 1995 by Ruth Heller. Grosset & Dunlap, Inc. Illustrations of chests on page 22 courtesy of Ruth Heller from *Merry-go-round: A Book about Nouns* by Ruth Heller. Copyright 1990 by Ruth Heller. Grosset & Dunlap, Inc. Illustration with text on bottom of page 22 from *Color* by Ruth Heller. Copyright 1995 by Ruth Heller. Putnam & Grosset. Permissions granted by G. P. Putnam's Sons, Putnam & Grosset Group. Illustration on page 23 from *The Korean Cinderella* by Shirley Climo, illustrated by Ruth Heller. Illustrations copyright 1993 by Ruth Heller. HarperCollins Children's Books. Illustration on page 20 from *King Solomon and the Bee* text adapted by Dalia Hardof Renberg, illustrated by Ruth Heller. Illustrations copyright 1994 by Ruth Heller. HarperCollins Children's Books. Permissions granted by HarperCollins Children's Books. Original illustration on page 11 by Ruth Heller. Puzzle books on page 13 by Ruth Heller. Copyright 1974 by Western Publishing Co. Inc. Books on page 13 Designs for Coloring, by Ruth Heller. Copyright 1976, 1978, 1979 by Grosset & Dunlap, Inc. Crossword puzzle on page 16 copyright SAN FRANCISCO CHRONICLE. Reprinted by permission. Picture of Yaddo on page 14 appears courtesy of Yaddo, Saratoga Springs, NY.